IN THE PRESENCE OF
THE DRAGON THRONE

Ch'ing Dynasty Costume (1644-1911)
in the Royal Ontario Museum

by John E. Vollmer

Publication of this book has been
made possible by grants from
Simpsons, Limited
and
Simpsons-Sears Limited
Toronto, Canada

ROM

Royal Ontario Museum
Toronto, Canada

Copyright © 1977 by the Royal
Ontario Museum
ISBN 0-88854-195-3

Catalogue design by Newton & Frank
Associates Inc.
Drawings by T. Allom, engraved
by J.B. Allen from Rev. G.N.
Wright, *The Chinese Empire
historical and descriptive
illustrating the manners and
customs of the Chinese*, London,
London Printing and Publishing
Co. Ltd. (1843)
Typesetting by Howarth & Smith Ltd.
Printing and binding by Hunter Rose
Company
Printed and bound in Canada

Cover illustrations: A dragon badge
from an emperor's surcoat, 1850-1875
914.7.8
Photo by W. Robertson, ROM

CONTENTS

"Rice Sellers at the Military Station of Tong-Chang-foo"

ACKNOWLEDGMENTS

This study would not have been possible without the faith of the late Harold B. Burnham, former head of the Textile Department, who invited me to join his staff in 1970 and placed the vast East Asian collections under my responsibility. I am particularly indebted to my colleague, Dorothy K. Burnham, whose work on garment construction and its relationship to technology and raw materials has shaped my thinking on this problem. Her encouragement and counsel have resulted in many of the explorations and conclusions forwarded here. Omissions and inaccuracies are, of course, my own responsibility.

For special assistance with this manuscript, I wish to thank Dr. Hsio-yen Shih, Curator of the Far Eastern Department, Dr. Doris J. Dohrenwend, Assistant Curator of the Far Eastern Department, Dr. Veronika Gervers, Associate Curator of the Textile Department, and Dr. R.L. Peterson, Curator of the Mammalogy Department. I also wish to acknowledge the help given by G. Christine Manville, who prepared material for the map from various Russian sources, and by David Pepper and Julian Mulock, who prepared final drawings from my rough sketches.

John E. Vollmer
December 1976

Mongolia

Manchuria

Amur River

Gobi Desert

Jehol
Peking

Tibetan Plateau

Himalaya Mountains

Huang (Yellow) River

China

Nanking

Yangtzu River

Pearl River

Canton

Eastern Asia

∿∿∿∿	Great Wall
– – –	Extent of Ch'ing Dynasty China
··········	Present National Boundaries
⌄⌄⌄	Manchu Territory Prior to 1600
≡≡≡	Steppe (sagebrush and grassland)
·:·:·	Oak Forest
░░░	Spruce, Fir, Larch Forest

▨▨▨	Desert
∴∴∴	High Plateau, Woodland
▦▦▦	Subtropical Forest
─·─·─	Tropical Forest
▥▥▥	Semi-Arid Steppe ("Puszta")

CHRONOLOGY

**Yuan Dynasty 1260-1368
(Mongol)**

Ming Dynasty 1368-1644

**Ch'ing Dynasty 1644-1911
(Manchu)**

Manchu Emperors

Nuerhaci (T'ai-tsu) 1559–1626

Abahai (T'ai-tsung) 1626–1643

Shun-chih 1644–1662

K'ang-hsi 1662–1723

Yung-cheng 1723–1736

Ch'ien-lung 1736–1796

Chia-ch'ing 1796–1821

Tao-kuang 1821–1851

Hsien-feng 1851–1862

T'ung-chih 1862–1875

Kuang-hsü 1875–1908

Hsüan-t'ung 1908–1911

CLOTHING AND THE POLITICS OF CONQUEST

In 1644 a small band of nomadic warriors from Manchuria conquered China. Declaring their right to the Dragon Throne, the Manchu named their dynasty Ch'ing (Pure) and ruled until 1911, when, under the pressures of internal decline and external threat, the dynasty collapsed, bringing imperial China to an end. The effects of conquest by a people ethnically and culturally different from the Chinese were manifold. The Manchu brought with them a structured military organization which ensured the separation of conqueror and conquered, and a strong nomadic heritage which differed significantly from the Chinese agrarian way of life. The Manchu were aware that the many nomadic conquerors who had preceded them had eventually been assimilated by the Chinese. To prevent a similar fate, they developed a political organization sufficient to maintain the Chinese style bureaucracy while at the same time maintaining their own identity.

To counter the threat of sinification, the Manchu stressed various cultural attributes that would emphasize their ethnic differences. Among the simplest differences to maintain were language and custom; probably the most visual distinction was costume. They changed the court attire from the ample, flowing robes and slippers with upturned toes of the sedentary Ming to the boots, trousers, and functional riding coats of nomadic horsemen, a simple but emphatic gesture. The queue and the Manchu national dress thus became symbols of the authority of a small group of nomadic warriors ruling over a much larger Chinese population. By imposing their national costume on all

in government service, the Manchu acknowledged their steppe origins and legitimized their claims to rule by linking the Ch'ing Dynasty with the other nomadic dynasties which had preceded them.

The aim of this catalogue is twofold: to introduce the ROM's magnificent Chinese costume collection to a larger audience, and to trace various aspects of the origins and development of Ch'ing period costume. It focuses on the cultural and social history of costume as well as its political significance.

Traditional garments embody the continuity of a people's life style, its social morés, cultural values, and technological developments. Change in clothing is bound up with psychological and philosophical considerations, and is seldom achieved without external influence. In part people derive their identity from the clothing they wear. Kinship and rank, political function, and social occasion are frequently denoted by a particular costume deemed acceptable by a peer group. Deviation from the norm implies an alteration of identity.

Studies of costume history should distinguish between garment constructions and style. Construction is the basic factor determining costume shapes; style is more superficial. Changes in garment construction are most often an evolution of, not a radical departure from, tradition. Technological, social, or cultural developments may effect gradual changes which are often almost imperceptible over long periods of time. Even the more dramatic influences such as war, migration, or industrialization may not have an immediate effect on traditional garment constructions. Frequently some simple modification to a basic garment structure may persist long after the reasons for its original development have been forgotten.

Style, however, is a subtle thing, sensitive to changes in taste, status, or rank. It frequently involves only minor variations such as changes in colour, material, decoration, or manner of wearing the garment. Quite often style functions independently of construction. Style may be linked to timeliness and is often related to class, rank, ethnic origin, or political affiliation.

Traditional garments often serve as the collective memory of a people's history. By tracing developments in garment construction and style, costume history can enable us to appreciate and possibly to better understand past cultures.

"The Great Wall of China"

HISTORICAL BACKGROUND

The Great Wall stretches in a vast arc across China's northern frontier. Built as a defence system to protect the agricultural basis of China's high urban culture from the intrusions of nomadic barbarians, it was more a symbol of power than an effective deterrent to invasion. South and east of this barrier, on the central Chinese plains, agriculture made sedentary urban existence possible; to the north and west, breeders of horses, sheep, and cattle were obliged to live as nomads following their herds in search of forage on the rolling steppe.

Beyond the eastern extremity of the Great Wall, where it touches the sea at Shanhaikuan, lies an area of northern Asia which has been home to peoples who repeatedly threatened and, on occasion, subjugated the inhabitants of the Chinese plains. Among them were the Manchu.

The name, Manchuria, is a twentieth-century invention identifying a political reality; but historically this area bore no specific name, having neither defined borders nor uniform population. Geographically, it consists of three regions. Although separate, these regions overlapped; the zones of contact and interaction were not static. The first, lying just outside the Great Wall, was the northernmost extension of the territory which maintained Chinese agrarian life. Here, the agrarian economy led to a Chinese life style and bureaucratic government. The area served as a political buffer zone between farmer and herder; through it passed routes of communication between China proper and the tribute-paying barbarians. Despite the Chinese presence, the area was isolated and vulnerable, particularly in times of waning central control and ascendancy of nomadic power.

To the west and the northwest are the easternmost extensions of the steppes which stretch across Asia. These grasslands supported nomadic societies of tribal peoples who lived in felt tents and bred horses, sheep, and cattle.

Further north the grasslands give way to the spruce and larch forests of eastern Siberia. Here the environment imposes another type of nomadism. In an arc extending north to east, the forests and marshes of the Amur River drainage contained the hunting and fishing nomads of Tungus origin. Reindeer were used for transportation in the north; dog sled and canoe to the east; and in areas of Chinese contact the horse was used.

The pig was the chief domestic animal and in later historical times a desultory agriculture was practised.

Chinese culture developed at points of contact between the distinct geographic and climatic zones of steppe and plains. From prehistoric times farmer and herder were in conflict. Farming tied up free range land; while herding destroyed fields, crops, and irrigation systems. Yet agriculture provided the economic support for the developing high urban culture and also the luxuries so coveted by the nomad.

The nomadic way of life fostered vigorous independence and militancy, and Chinese dynastic history reflects the resulting conflict between the nomads and the sedentary plains dwellers. In periods of empire, with strong native dynasties on the throne, China extended the limits of control onto the southern edge of the steppe; but when central control weakened, nomadic groups repeatedly were able to consolidate power, using their mounted cavalry to seize control and establish their own dynasties on the throne. In the third century the Turkic-speaking Hsiung-nu or Asiatic Huns brought the weakened Han empire to an end. Later, the mighty T'ang empire collapsed before the Mongol Khitans, who established the Liao Dynasty in northern China in A.D. 907, only to be replaced by the Tungus Jurched in the twelfth century. In the thirteenth century the Mongols swept into southern China to establish the Yuan Dynasty and were overturned when the native Ming Dynasty was founded in 1368.

The ancestors of the Manchu were the hunting and fishing nomads of Tungus origin, who, by the seventeenth century, had been completely transformed into a steppe herder society. The development of the Manchu state can be traced to a small frontier group, holding a favourable political and trade position in eastern Manchuria, who were formed into a feudal administrative unit by the Ming Chinese. The founder of the state, Nuerhaci (1559–1626), began his career within a world of feudal rivalry. Called to leadership after his father's murder, Nuerhaci had to secure his own position against his chief rival, another Manchu nobleman, who had caused the death of Nuerhaci's father and grandfather on a looting raid conducted with Chinese support. In destroying his rival Nuerhaci opposed Chinese frontier officials, pitting himself and his followers against the Ming state. Throughout the late sixteenth and early seventeenth century, Nuerhaci secured an ever larger territorial base and consolidated Manchu power north of the Great Wall.

The Manchu conquest began on the margins of the Chinese world. Gradually the Manchu accepted a Chinese style administrative organization to manage the area of Chinese agriculture and its sedentary population. This area had repeatedly served as the economic base for all political organization in northern Asia, and control of this rich income area was essential if nomadic conquest of the plains was to be attempted. The Manchu followed an age-old pattern of learning Chinese administration on a small scale before subjugating the empire, and their political organization grew as they penetrated further and further into the Chinese plains.

Abahai, Nuerhaci's son, succeeded to power in 1626 and during the second quarter of the century brought the remaining Chinese parts of Manchuria under control. By increasing the numbers of Chinese troops and officials in the Manchu ranks he further transformed the Manchu government and gained control of the Mongol tribes to the west. In 1635 the name Manchu was first used and the dynastic title, Ch'ing, was adopted to signify the Manchu determination to make their own claim to the Dragon Throne. Earlier they had called their dynasty Hou Chin or Later Chin, in reference to the Chin Dynasty (1115-1234) of the Jurched tribes from whom the Manchu claimed descent. Abahai died in 1643. A year later inner disorder and decay brought about the collapse of the Ming Dynasty, giving the Manchu regent, Dorgon, the chance to place the infant Shun-chih on the Dragon Throne.

Much of the success of the Manchu conquest rested upon an internal organization which permitted them to effect the transition from nomadic conquerors to civil administrators. In 1601 Nuerhaci organized all Manchu troops into companies of three hundred warriors; five companies formed a battalion. These in turn were grouped into four large units called banners, distinguished by their yellow, white, red, and blue flags. Enrolment of an individual warrior into the banner system extended to include his family. From the outset the banner system provided effective military discipline and a comprehensive register of civilians, monitoring the Manchu population and guaranteeing

the equitable distribution of lands and taxes that ensured the livelihood of its members.

As the ranks increased during the first decades of the seventeenth century, Nuerhaci continued to develop new companies and attached them to various banners. In 1615 he created four more banners, making a total of eight. The new banners were distinguished by flags of the original colours with contrasting borders. Manchu ranks were also increased by Chinese who switched loyalties and by alliances with various Mongol tribes. By 1634 eight separate Mongol banners had been created, followed in 1642 by eight Chinese banners.

The head of each banner was a lieutenant-general appointed from the imperial clan who was responsible for both civil and military affairs. In the formative period these clansmen formed a council to advise the ruler; but as the size and complexity of the state grew, an administrative structure developed to match the military one. By the second quarter of the seventeenth century executive power was concentrated in the person of the emperor and his immediate family. Deliberative bodies were appointed to facilitate internal management (grand secretariat, censor, inner departments) and external administration (colonial affairs). In addition, boards responsible for civil affairs, finance, rites, war, justice, and public works were established, patterned on Chinese models. The large number of Chinese officials already within the Manchu ranks influenced the formation of Manchu bureaucracy. Once the Manchu government was in place in Peking, the Hanlin Academy, with its time-honoured examination system based on Confucian learning and notions of statecraft, continued to supply the necessary scholar-officials for these numerous administrative positions. To deter Chinese elitism and lessen the threat of assimilation of non–Chinese, the Manchu instituted a quota system to limit the number of Chinese degree-holders in the bureaucracy.

Paralleling, and in some instances superseding, the elaborate hierarchy established in the civil and military bureaucracies was an aristocratic hierarchy based on clan affiliation. In addition to belonging to a banner organization which held him in a fixed pyramidal position loyal to an autocratic emperor, every Manchu was also a member of a clan in which his position was fixed by kinship. Each clan group owed feudal allegiance to the imperial clan and its paternal leader, who was also the emperor. Imperial clansmen, the heads of the imperial household and bodyguard, lieutenant-generals of the Manchu banners, and chief metropolitan officers were held together by rank and inherited privilege to form a Manchu elite. Probably numbering no more than 2,000, this group wielded the power of an autonomous government against the overwhelming forces of Chinese culture.

Successful government relied on an efficient bureaucracy which organized thousands of individuals into an elaborately graded structure that related in all of its functions to the emperor. Distinctions of title, rank, and status in the imperial court in metropolitan and provincial administrations, as well as in the military organizations, were in no little part furthered by the prescribed costume and paraphernalia worn by each courtier, official, and officer in service of the Dragon Throne.

"Destroying the Chrysalides and reeling the [silk] Cocoons"

EAST ASIAN CLOTHING TRADITIONS

Most studies of Far Eastern costume have been concerned with tracing the evolution of styles in attempts to establish chronology. Others have described garment types to distinguish regional groups. Few have dealt with costume technology as it relates to both origin and development of styles. In eastern Asia, these do not necessarily coincide with fixed dynastic periods or recognized geographical regions.

Costume technology underscores the complex relationships between steppe and plains societies as they relate to the development of East Asian culture. From literary sources and historical data it is possible to distinguish two costume styles within Ch'ing period China. Although a Manchu style can be isolated from a Chinese style, when examining actual garments it is impossible to discuss one without reference to the other. Style is frequently equated with shape; but little attention has been given to the reason why those shapes exist, or, even more fundamentally, how they are constructed. Although nomadic garments based on skin constructions contrast with Chinese cloth constructions, the surviving ethnographical evidence demonstrates a long period of interaction between them.

Manchu garments were the most recent nomadic influence imposed upon traditional China. At the time of conquest the Chinese had already adopted many nomadic garments, naturalizing them as part of Chinese national costume. Trousers and paired aprons worn informally by Chinese women since at least the second century B.C. relate directly to the formal Manchu male court coats. Both undoubtedly derived from a common general source, although each represents a separate line of development.

Both steppe and plain traditions are represented in Ch'ing Dynasty costume, but neither the nomadic Manchu style nor the agrarian Chinese style existed in isolation. Chinese cultural history has been interpreted in terms of recurring cycles of native development and nomadic intrusion, but care must be taken not to polarize these influences. Nomadic and agrarian traditions are only two aspects of a larger phenomenon.

Chinese Continuity

The emergence of an organized agrarian society on the central Chinese plains at the close of the Neolithic period imposed a sedentary life style and encouraged the growth of large urban centres. The emerging Chinese empire required an efficient bureaucracy to manage administrative details and it eventually became the dominant political and cultural force within eastern Asia. Within this sphere of influence men were either civilized and Chinese or barbarians. Despite changes of political leadership, a life style tied to the land and a cultural tradition which valued the past continued to impose uniformity and insulated China against change.

Within eastern Asia garments are most commonly made of cloth. Weaving in China can be traced back to the second millennium B.C. through the silk and hemp textile remains preserved in the patinas of bronze objects found in Shang Dynasty (c.1600–1028 B.C.) burials. From the late Chou Dynasty (fourth-fifth centuries B.C.) and the Han Dynasty (206 B.C.–A.D. 220) there is an ever-increasing body of archaeological data and literary record which documents Chinese weaving and garment constructions. Artistic representations provide additional evidence for many garment types which do not survive.

From at least the second millennium B.C., silk was the pre-eminent fibre for luxury garments. Silk was used extensively in diplomacy and commerce as early as the fifth century B.C. and reached Rome in the first century B.C.; though China's secrets of sericulture were not known in the West until the Middle Ages. Hemp and other bast fibres were used during the Neolithic period and probably formed the basis of most non-aristocratic clothing until cotton, introduced from India, became widely available in the twelfth century. Wool was noticeably absent in China and belonged instead to the nomadic herders, who always possessed some source of animal hair with which to make felt.

In eastern Asia, narrow backstrap looms were used which produced cloth of insufficient width to cover the body in a single length. As a result, all upper body garments had a centre back seam and were formed of two lengths of material brought over the shoulder, leaving the front open, in the familiar kimono construction. Sleeves were additional lengths of material joined to the sides at the shoulder. With this construction the sleeve functions independently of the body of the garment and can be extended in length or width to almost any dimension. Additional fabric sewn on to the front edges provided overlap for more secure closure and better body covering.

Technological improvements of later historical periods increased the loom width, but did not alter the traditional centre back seam construction. From our earliest evidence this

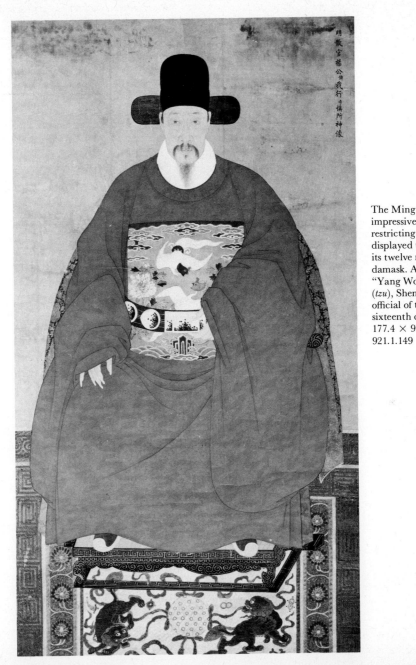

The Ming Dynasty *p'ao* coat was an impressive court garment. While restricting movement, it dramatically displayed the wealth represented by its twelve metres of lustrous silk damask. Ancestor portrait inscribed "Yang Wo-hsing, official pseudonym (*tzu*), Shen Shou, honourific palace official of the Ming [Dynasty]". Late sixteenth century.
177.4 × 97.8 cm
921.1.149

The full sleeves of this woman's embroidered silk gauze coat place it emphatically within cloth traditions, in which conspicuous displays of woven cloth reflect wealth and status. 1850-1875.
950.100.532 Krenz collection, gift of Mrs. Sigmund Samuel

Although the front closing of this blue silk damask coat has been modified in a Manchu style, the emphasis on contrasting borders and bindings is characteristic of Chinese aesthetics. Embroidered in silk and couched gold filé. 1875-1900.
970.76.2 gift of Mrs. Percyval Tudor-Hart

Cloth coat with centre back seam construction, from a nineteenth-century Korean man's hemp mourning coat (ROM 915.3.99) preserving the *p'ao* court coat of the Han through T'ang dynasties.

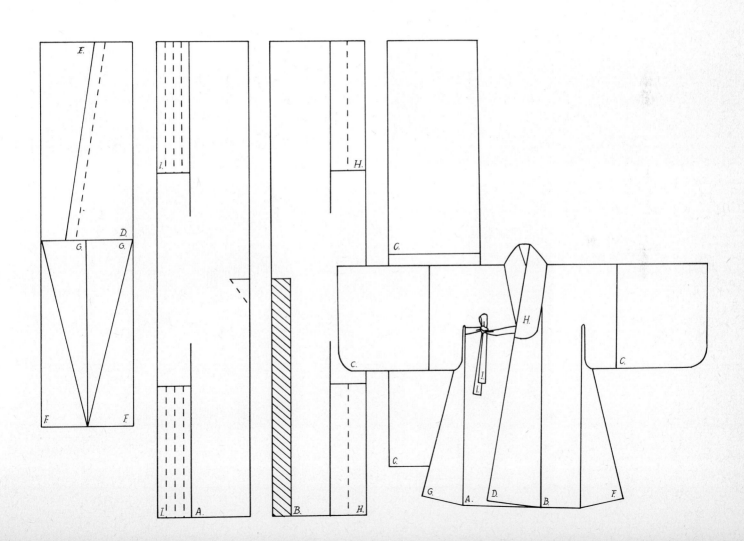

The feathered and jewelled sections attached to the lattice base of formal Chinese women's hats imitate masses of ornamental hairpins arranged in an upswept coiffure. 1875-1900. 922.4.41

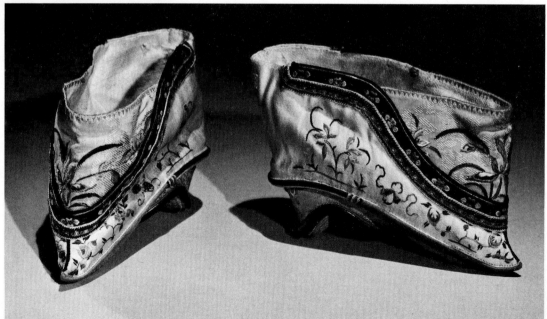

Women's feet were bound in order to deform their growth, as small feet were a mark of status within Chinese society. Tiny embroidered shoes such as these were worn on "lotus bud" feet of upper-class women. About 1900. 972.413.1 gift of Mrs. C.M. Warren

kimono construction has served both ceremonial and practical roles. As full-length coats made of luxurious silk, they enhanced the court ritual of an autocratic state. Reduced to their basic form, they were the occupational garment of farm labourers.

From ancient times the *p'ao* coat, resembling a kimono with wide sleeves, was used for formal wear. Its form was codified during the Han Dynasty, and each succeeding native dynasty attempted to restore this classic form to stress continuity and to evoke the grandeur of the past. When the Ming overthrew the Mongol Yuan Dynasty in 1368, they again restored the *p'ao*, rejecting the close-fitting coats of the Mongols. As its skirts were widened with additional widths of cloth at the sides, and its sleeves extended enormously in width and length, the *p'ao* became impressive in its bulk and lavish use of silk. At the time of the Manchu conquest the extremely generous cut of the Ming court coat required over twelve metres of silk. Such a heavy coat encumbered movement, imposing a slow and orderly pace appropriate to court pageantry. The sleeves honoured the Chinese aversion to displaying the hands in public on formal occasions and had the practical merit of significantly reducing the threat of assassination. After the Manchu invasion, variants

of this full-cut coat were retained in areas of Chinese society that were unaffected by official Manchu regulation. Informal wear, bridal attire, and coats made to clothe temple images continued to follow Chinese tradition.

Traditional Chinese footwear was based on lacquered wooden clogs or on rigid sole sandals, the latter often converted to a slipper by the addition of cloth uppers.

Occupational headgear was based on a circular sunshade, usually plaited of straw or bamboo. The conical sunshade was adopted by the Manchu court as official summer attire. Chinese women's formal hats imitated elaborate coiffeurs. Men's formal hats were commonly rigid affairs resembling bonnets with stiffened streamers projecting perpendicularly at the back, possibly evoking a scarf tied at the back of the head over a high chignon.

The Nomadic Heritage

Nomadic steppe peoples occupied an area between two garment-making traditions. To the south, sedentary populations developed weaving technology as early as the second

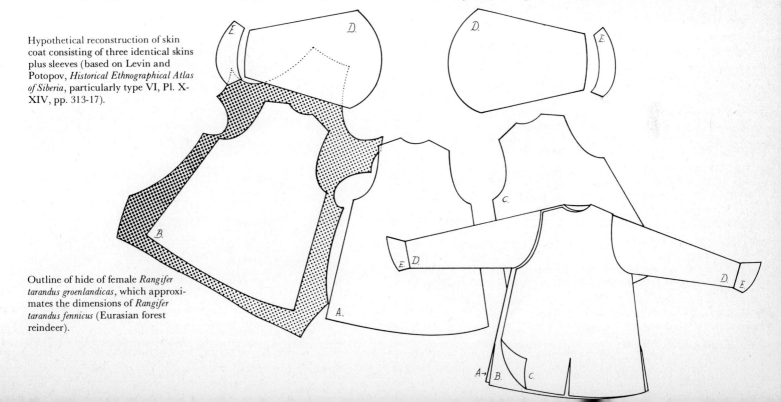

Hypothetical reconstruction of skin coat consisting of three identical skins plus sleeves (based on Levin and Potopov, *Historical Ethnographical Atlas of Siberia*, particularly type VI, Pl. X-XIV, pp. 313-17).

Outline of hide of female *Rangifer tarandus groenlandicas*, which approximates the dimensions of *Rangifer tarandus fennicus* (Eurasian forest reindeer).

millennium B.C. and used woven cloth as the basis of garment constructions. In the forested areas to the north, clothing material was provided by animal skins acquired by hunting or trapping. Both traditions reflect the notion of economy and the optimum use of available raw material. As the physical dimensions of skin and cloth differ, approaches to garment constructions vary. Skin dimensions are limited to the size of the animal. Although irregular in shape, skins have a definite symmetry and grain which can be exploited to fashion garments from them. Woven cloth is generally of unlimited length but of a fixed width determined by the type of weaving equipment employed. The rectilinear properties of cloth result in the straight seams and geometric shapes of cloth constructions.

Whenever the raw materials of one culture are adopted by another culture to make garments, concessions are the inevitable result. Often, construction principles of the original tradition are so strongly entrenched in a life style or culture that principles of economy are sacrificed for matters of style. The garments of horseriding herders evolved from the skin traditions developed by the forest-dwelling hunting and fishing nomads of the north. Whether through conquest or commerce, contact with the cloth traditions of the southern agrarian peoples affected northern garment construction. When woven cloth was introduced with all its limitations and variables, garment construction on the steppe underwent some radical changes, but the memory of the skin tradition was never entirely eradicated. Even when life styles and cultures underwent fundamental transformation, such as took place when the Manchu moved from the steppe to the palaces of the Forbidden City, the old clothing traditions continued to be honoured.

At the time of conquest the Manchu possessed a costume which had evolved from their nomadic life style. Manchu costume is closely related to the basic costume of horseriding herdsmen living on or adjacent to the eastern part of the Eurasian steppe. Function, raw materials, concerns for protection from exposure, and ease of manoeuvrability were the chief determinants of garment shapes.

Whether long or short, the horseman's coat was designed for movement and a life outdoors. Closely fitting the upper body with long, tight sleeves and usually belted at the waist, the coat helped conserve body heat, while giving free arm movement for riding or for conducting military operations from horseback.

A Manchu warrior is depicted in one
of fifty commemorative portraits
honouring meritorious officers who
pacified Tibet by imperial command.
He wears clothing evolved from
horseriding herders. Dated to 1760.
153 × 94.6 cm
925x84.4

Although made of blue silk velvet,
neither the style nor the cut of this
short sleeveless coat is based on cloth
constructions. Its prototype is probably a two-skin garment. 1875-1900.
958x104

The lower part of the coat was slashed or vented to prevent it from bunching at the waist when the rider was seated in the saddle. Long, tight sleeves prevented the wind from blowing up the arm and were often cut generously long so they could be pulled down to cover the hand. Flaring sleeve extensions, such as the characteristic Manchu horsehoof cuff *(ma-ti hsiu)*, offered further protection for the back of the hand.

The extreme overlap of the left front extension to the opposite side seam characteristic of Manchu and Manchu-influenced coats is the most eastern variant of methods of closing the coat tightly at the neck. Toggle button and loop arrangements to secure the flap derived from skin traditions. The curved shape

of the flap echoes the contour of an animal skin, not the straight lines characteristic of rectilinear woven cloth.

Sleeveless coats, always worn over long-sleeved coats, were typical of regions along the northern frontiers of China. Most ethnographical examples of the garment were worn exclusively by women, often on festive or formal occasions. Superficially the sleeveless coat appears similar to coat constructions, only made without sleeves. However, this does not explain the prevalence of sloping shoulder seams, for in all East Asian cloth traditions narrow widths of fabric are sewn longitudinally to form coats without shoulder seams. The form of the sleeveless coat, therefore, strongly suggests the survival of an archaic upper

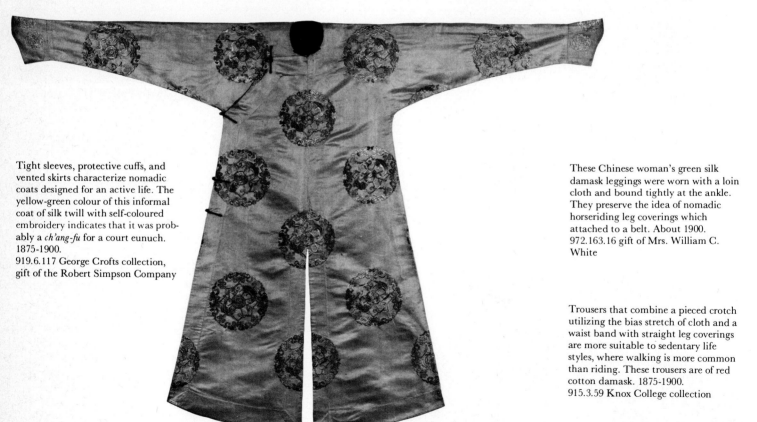

Tight sleeves, protective cuffs, and vented skirts characterize nomadic coats designed for an active life. The yellow-green colour of this informal coat of silk twill with self-coloured embroidery indicates that it was probably a *ch'ang-fu* for a court eunuch. 1875-1900.
919.6.117 George Crofts collection, gift of the Robert Simpson Company

These Chinese woman's green silk damask leggings were worn with a loin cloth and bound tightly at the ankle. They preserve the idea of nomadic horseriding leg coverings which attached to a belt. About 1900.
972.163.16 gift of Mrs. William C. White

Trousers that combine a pieced crotch utilizing the bias stretch of cloth and a waist band with straight leg coverings are more suitable to sedentary life styles, where walking is more common than riding. These trousers are of red cotton damask. 1875-1900.
915.3.59 Knox College collection

body garment formed of three skins: one for the back and two for the front. This basic construction is typical of skin garments of southeastern Siberia. The overlap of the two skins provided additional warmth and protection for the front of the body and would have been a particularly effective shield against the wind for a horseman. Simple lacings at the shoulders and under the arm would have held the garment in place. The substitution of pairs of ties or toggles and loops along one shoulder and side seam would have permitted the garment to be taken off and put on with a minimum of adjustment. All recent ethnographical examples made of cloth utilize this means of closure, and most have a minimum of side seams that produce deep vents even when the garment is extended full-length.

The sleeveless coat by itself was not a practical garment for the steppe environment, since some form of arm covering is essential for most outdoor activities. Certain nomadic attitudes exhibited in modes of wearing sleeved coats strongly suggest that sleeves may once have been auxiliary to the basic upper body garment. For instance, when long outer sleeves encumber arm movements, such as in archery, rather than removing the coat the wearer frequently disengaged his arm, allowing the sleeve to hang at the back or tucking it into the belt. Many of the degenerate sleeve forms found in Turkic coats of the western regions of the steppe may be a result of such attitudes. Retention of the less sophisticated variant for women's wear probably had to do with the division of labour by sex found within herder societies, where long sleeves would have hampered women in many of their camp-based occupations. Removing a separate sleeve entirely would have been simpler than pushing it back or rolling it up. Horsemen, on the other hand, would probably have preferred the warmth of a closed armhole when riding across the steppe and would have had no place to put a removable sleeve.

Adaptation of the sleeveless coat to cloth constructions presented problems. The angled shoulder seam construction is basic to many skin coats of southern Siberia, and even to some of the cloth coats from Mongolia as well as from those more western reaches of the Eurasian steppe. The original shape of the skin naturally created a sloping shoulder line and the curved armhole. But to achieve the same effect in cloth meant cutting away and wasting cloth. Accordingly, sleeved coats adapted to principles evolved from the cloth tradition largely superseded the sleeveless upper body garment in many East Asian cultures. Yet the nomadic memory persisted in valuing

Paired yellow satin aprons borrowed
from nomadic herder traditions
concealed Chinese women's trousers
and created the more impressive bulk
associated with formality. Only the
lower section exposed below the
three-quarter-length coat is embroidered. 1875-1900.
972.163.3 gift of Mrs. William C.
White

the older, more traditional form and eventually it was given a ceremonial position as an outer garment.

Trousers provided a horseman's legs with protection from the elements and from rubbing against the horse's flanks. Male leg coverings probably evolved from animal skins wrapped around the legs. A more permanent garment results when a seam replaces bindings or lacings. Examples of this form in cloth with provision for attachment to a belt and ties to bind it closely at the ankle survived in China into the twentieth century. Tubular constructions of cloth sewn to a waistband make a more convenient garment and true trousers are created by merging loin cloth and leggings.

One of the more outstanding Chinese borrowings from the steppe nomads is the use of trousers by both men and women. Official histories record that in 307 B.C. the ruler of the small state of Chao introduced mounted archers into his army. Not only did this ruler adopt a nomadic method of warfare, but he went so far as to insist that nomadic trousers and short coats be worn at his court, his reasons being that the Chinese style coat was too voluminous and clumsy to be practical. This innovation did not survive the weight of court custom, but nomadic costume was retained for basic military and occupational clothing. During the Ch'ing period, trousers and leggings continued to be worn informally by Chinese of both sexes and of all classes. Standard female attire consisted of trousers and the full-sleeved, three-quarter-length coat.

A second nomadic garment, a pair of aprons, was added to conceal the women's trousers on more formal occasions. Originally, paired aprons added the required sedentary dignity without hindering the movements of the wearer should the need arise to make a hasty getaway on horseback. The Chinese form from the post-Han period consisted of two identical pleated parts. By the Ming period and continuing throughout the Ch'ing Dynasty, each part consisted of a straight panel with a pleated section to the left. The straight panels were arranged at the centre front and back with the pleated sections flaring gracefully at the sides. Decoration was commonly concentrated across the lower section that remained exposed under the coat worn with it.

Boots were common foot coverings essential for both riding and camp-based herding on foot. Boots also stem from the skin tradition, combining skin leggings or stockings with either a moccasin-type sole which wraps around the foot or the more rigid layered sole which stops at the edge of the foot as a sandal. The soft moccasin type is more typical of the extreme eastern

Rigid soled boots permitted archers to stand in the stirrups while riding, greatly increasing the effectiveness of mounted attack. These velvet-trimmed black satin boots have soles layered of stiffened cotton and leather. About 1900.
922.4.84

part of Siberia, while the rigid sole type is more common on the steppe itself from Manchuria to Central Asia.

Hoods were commonly worn as a separate outer garment. These possibly were derived from close-fitting head coverings fashioned from the skins of actual animal heads, a form found repeatedly in circumpolar areas. On the eastern steppe the typical form, close-fitting at the crown and elongated at the back and sides with a fastening under the chin, covers the head as well as protects the ears and back of the neck. Its form is characterized by a vertical seam running from forehead to the back of the neck that joins identical halves. The basis of the Manchu official winter court hat was a close-fitting cap with rounded crown, made of wedge-shaped sections, with a separately attached upturned brim faced with fur which originally could be turned down for warmth.

The close-fitting inner hood of quilted blue cotton protects the head and neck from drafts; the outer hoop and flap of red wool broadcloth provide additional insulation and protection from inclement weather. 1850-1875. 915.3.145 Knox College collection

"Western Gate, Peking"

From the outset the Manchu distinguished their dynasty from the Chinese tradition by imposing the wearing of the queue and Manchu national dress by all in the service of the Ch'ing government. In the mid-eighteenth century this decision was codified in a comprehensive set of regulations commissioned by the Ch'ien-lung emperor to govern official costume and to guard against abuses in the interests of individual status. The *Huang-ch'ao li-ch'i t'u shih,* or Illustrated Catalogue of Ritual Paraphernalia of the Ch'ing Dynasty, contained strict regulations for all costume and accessories required for court ceremony. More importantly, it reiterated the rights of the conqueror as a check against increasing pressures to restore native Chinese costume. The reasons are eloquently summarized in the Ch'ien-lung preface:

"We, accordingly, have followed the old traditions of our dynasty, and have not dared to change them fearing that later men would hold us responsible for this, and criticize us regarding the robes and hats; and thus we would offend our ancestors. This we certainly should not do. Moreover, as for the Northern Wei, the Liao, and the Chin as well as the Yuan, all of which changed to Chinese robes and hats, they all died out within one generation [of abandoning their native dress]. Those of Our sons and grandsons who would take Our will as their will shall certainly not be deceived by idle talk. In this way the continuing Mandate of our dynasty will receive the protection of Heaven for ten thousand years. Do not change our traditions or reject them. Beware! Take warning!"

Portrait of I-lan t'ai, captain in the Mongol plain white banner, commemorating his elevation to fourth rank by imperial order. He wears the *ch'ao-fu* and *p'i-ling* collar with court accessories. Dated to 1790.
187.3 × 100.2 cm
921.32.77

Ch'ao-fu

The *ch'ao-fu* was the most formal of Manchu court garments. It was worn at the most important court functions, those that centred around the principal annual sacrifices conducted by the emperor himself on behalf of the well-being of the empire. Because of its ceremonial significance it was the most conservative of Manchu garments introduced into China, preserving features distinctive to Manchu national costume worn prior to the conquest. It is the most common garment depicted in Ch'ing period ancestor portraits. Because it was used as burial robes for those honoured to wear it, it is the rarest type of coat surviving in collections (Fernald, *Chinese Court Costume,* p. 14).

The male court coat consists of two separate units. The upper part is a hip-length riding coat; below is a pair of aprons, similar to the pairs of pleated aprons worn informally by Chinese women. The aprons are arranged to overlap at the sides; the small tab at the lower right of the coat *(jen)* is undoubtedly the vestige of some earlier form of closure.

Throughout history steppe nomads have worn aprons over their other garments in order to create the more impressive bulk associated with festive or formal garments. These aprons

Man's embroidered dull blue silk twill
ch'ao-fu. 1875-1900.
952x106

Evolution of Man's Ch'ao-fu

a) Hypothetical cloth modification of skin coat prototype based on 50 cm fabric width.

Formal costume consisting of basic long-sleeved coat with supplemental surcoat and paired aprons.

a

b) Surcoat reconstructed from man's *ch'ao-fu* (ROM 950.100.568).

c) Pair of aprons of embroidered silk attached to single waistband with ties of different fabric, about 1750 (Victoria and Albert Museum, T251-1966).

b

c

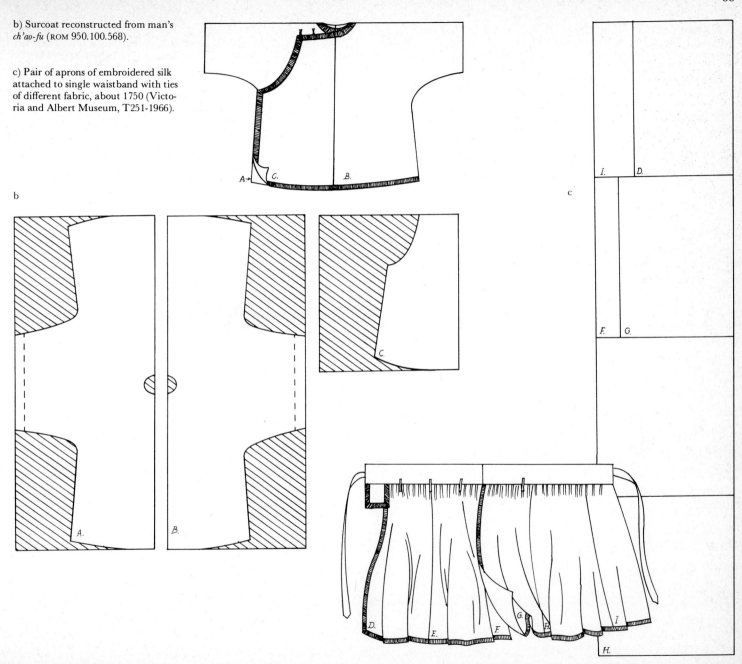

Codification of Male Ch'ao-fu

Cloth synthesis combining three
garments forming male court coat
from man's silk damask *ch'ao-fu* with
embroidered dragon insignia at chest
and back. 1875-1900 (ROM
950.100.568).

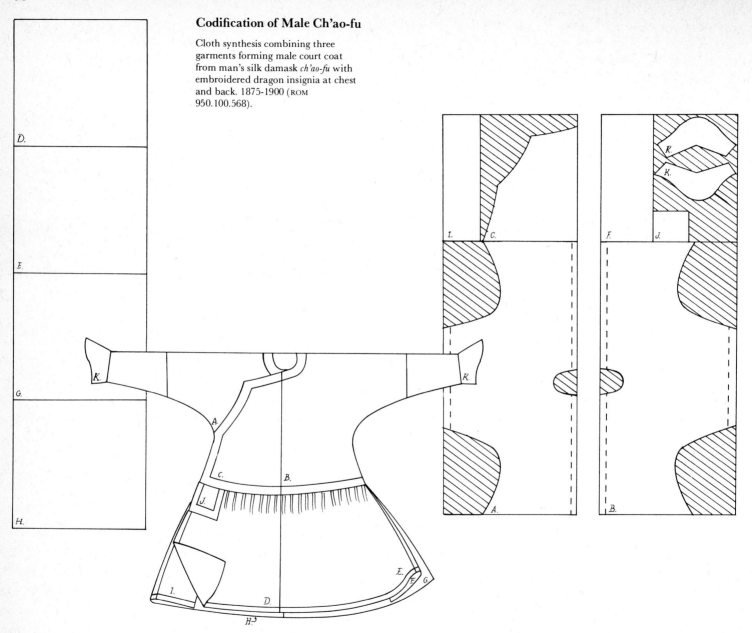

Evolution of Woman's Ch'ao-fu

a) Skin prototypes: long-sleeved coat
worn under full-length sleeveless coat.
b) Cloth synthesis combining the two,
applied bindings marking outlines of
original garments (note straight
shoulder line).
c) By 1759 a sleeveless coat opening
down the centre front with angled
shoulder line was added over the
ch'ao-fu.

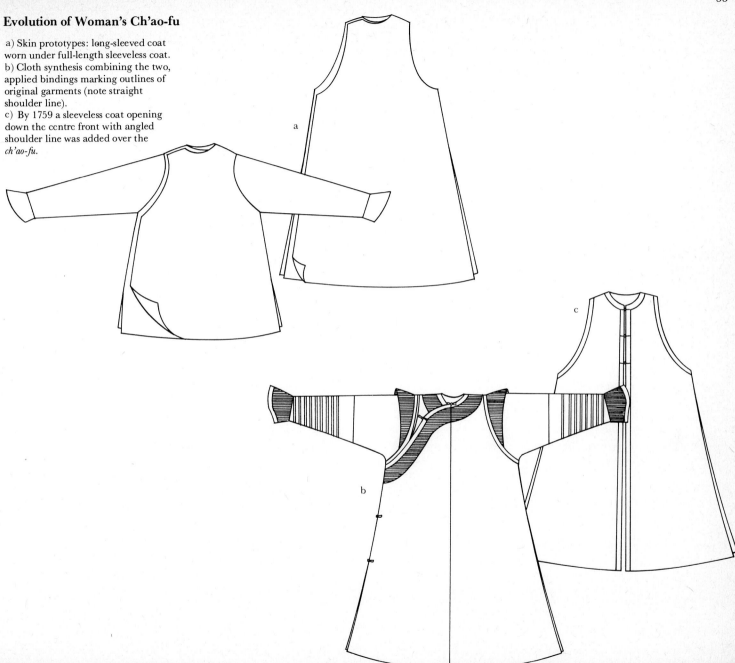

survived in costumes of many peoples living on or adjacent to the Eurasian steppe. Many of the more eastern variants which are characterized by pairs of identical aprons were in later times incorporated into skirts of coats, particularly among the Mongols and Manchu.

Most early Ch'ing depictions and all later surviving garments are these one-piece coats incorporating the short coat joined with two aprons. Evidence for the two-part garment remains in the construction. In the Victoria and Albert Museum is a mid-eighteenth-century pair of aprons in which the pair of pleated panels forming the skirts are attached to a single waistband; unfortunately the matching coat has not survived. At the end of the dynasty, when court regulations were no longer strictly enforced, lower-ranking courtiers frequently wore separate *ch'ao-fu* aprons over ordinary coats, under the surcoat bearing their insignia of rank, to save the expense of having a special court coat made (Cammann, *China's Dragon Robes,* p. 145).

The tight lower sleeves with horsehoof cuffs are of material that contrasts markedly with the rest of the coat, suggesting that two garments have evolved into a single unit. The characteristic Manchu sleeves are made of different fabric, most frequently black or dark blue which is either ribbed or patterned with sets of woven or embroidered bands. These retain a feature of the long, tight-fitting nomadic sleeves which extended over the hand, but which could be pushed up the arm in a series of parallel folds when the hand was engaged. An ornamental short-sleeved coat, worn over the more practical long-sleeved coat for formal occasions, has been used by many steppe cultures.

The typical decoration of dragon patterns, consisting of a large four-lobed yoke with a band of ornament at the hips and a dragon band across the skirts of the apron, does not really fit the garment's shape. It is the unsatisfactory result of adapting fabric designed for the earlier flowing Ming garment, which was based firmly in a cloth tradition, to the more restricted forms derived from skin traditions. As vassals of the Ming court, the leaders of the Manchu tribes received silks and dragon coats as diplomatic gifts in return for tribute. These bolts of presentation silks were in turn made up in local Manchu style; or, as Cammann argues, actual Ming coats were cut down. By the time of conquest the tradition of silk Manchu *ch'ao-fu* was so

firmly established that its form was considered inviolable. Throughout the dynasty the disposition of designs continued with only minor changes in style or placement. Being made of fine silk, the *ch'ao-fu* was suitable only for ceremonial wear; only in construction does it symbolize the function for which it was designed.

Although its form is debased and the importance of the original construction largely misunderstood, Manchu women's court attire reflects archaic features similar to those of male attire. The form is also based on a two-part garment: a long-sleeved, full-length coat with a full-length sleeveless coat worn over it. Probably by the time of conquest and certainly by the mid-eighteenth century when court costume was regulated by imperial edict, these two garments had merged into a single coat. Applied bindings and the flaring projections preserved the outline of the earlier sleeveless coat, whose function had ceased to have meaning.

By the mid-eighteenth century another element had been added to the woman's formal *ch'ao-fu*. This was a second sleeveless full-length coat on which were displayed insignia appropriate to rank. It opened down the front and was vented at the back. Although related to the Manchu's own sleeveless coat, this garment is actually traced through a Chinese development. Among formal clothing of the Ming Dynasty women wore narrow knee-length vests over their voluminous court coats. These vests were used to display insignia of rank. To accommodate the very wide Ming-style sleeves, the side seams were left open and the front and back sections were held together with straps. Although originally a type of sleeveless coat, before the end of the Ming period this garment had been so modified as to resemble a stole. When the Manchu court adopted the principle of pictorial devices to identify rank, it also adopted the vehicle for displaying it. The garment was again modified, and resumed the shape of a full-length sleeveless coat. Unofficial Chinese women's costume throughout the Ch'ing Dynasty continued to make use of the older Ming style court garment. Wide-sleeved coats of red silk, the favoured Ming colour, were worn for special family celebrations, particularly weddings. On such occasions the old Ming court vest, often trimmed with tasseled fringes, was worn.

Woman's court attire of the mid-
nineteenth century, including *ch'ao-fu*,
court vest, and *p'i-ling* collar. Ancestor
portrait of an unknown aristocratic
Manchu.
165.5 × 92.7 cm
921.1.142

Woman's pale orange silk tapestry-woven *ch'ao-fu*, probably for the
consort of the heir apparent (sleeves
altered). 1875-1900.
914.7.7

P'i-ling

Both male and female court coats were worn with separate triangular collars, *p'i-ling*, which flared over the shoulders at the back. The costume was considered incomplete without it. The shape and form of this flaring tippet resemble a separate hood, which when opened along the top of the crown would lie flat across the shoulders. If this hypothesis is true, then the garment is related to the larger family of steppe garments with back collars which convert into hoods (Gervers, *The Hungarian Szür*), rather than to the Chinese yoke or cloud collars called *yün-chien*

(Cammann, *China's Dragon Robes*, p. 135). The Manchu form had lost all vestiges of tabs or fringes which might once have served to tie the top together.

Ch'i-fu

Full-length, semi-formal coats called *ch'i-fu* were worn by all in attendance at court or in service of the Manchu imperial government and became the official Ch'ing period costume. They were far more common than the *ch'ao-fu*. They were made in much larger quantity, were worn by more officials, and

The silk tapestry-woven *p'i-ling* collar worn with Manchu court coats suggests a hood opened flat along the top seam. About 1900.
958.5 gift of Mrs. M. Brown

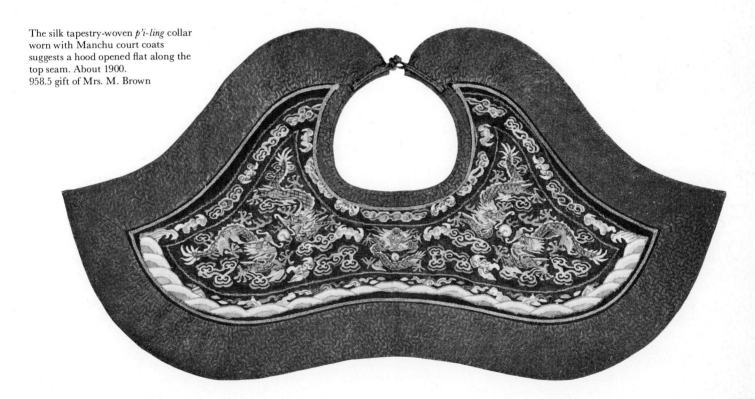

survive in larger numbers than any other article of court attire. The construction of the garment is based on the nomadic riding coat with its long, tight sleeves with horsehoof cuffs, its front flap which closed over the right with toggle buttons and loops, and the vented skirts which extended full-length for ceremonial display. This coat is commonly called a dragon robe after its principal ornament. The garment is among the clearest statements of Manchu intentions concerning the political and social functions of costume.

Although prototypes of the *ch'i-fu* can be traced to dragon-patterned semi-formal coats of preceding dynasties, the Manchu did not develop the *ch'i-fu* until after their conquest of China. The dragon was the paramount symbol of the Manchu period. It was used profusely to decorate objects worn or used by the imperial household as well as on objects used by those representing imperial authority. Just when the dragon became an imperial emblem in China is lost to memory. At least by the T'ang Dynasty (618-906), dragons decorated Chinese imperial coats. These are recorded as having only three claws. The Manchu reserved the five-clawed dragon *(lung)* for the emperor and his immediate family. Lesser nobles were obliged to use the four-clawed *mang* unless granted the privilege of wearing the imperial symbol.

The use of costume to further political aims is very ancient in China; but few garments in its long history have managed to demonstrate these intentions as clearly as the *ch'i-fu*. *Ch'i-fu* decoration was consciously designed to symbolize the concept of universal order, upon which the principles of Chinese imperial statecraft rested. The basic decorative schema was transmitted from Ming period ornament. In the decoration found on the yoke and horizontal bands decorating the skirts of Ming court coats are the elements of Chinese cosmology. At first, as vassals of the Ming court, the Manchu had borrowed the outward forms of these symbols for their own garments; later, as rulers of the Central Kingdom, they embraced the spirit and substance of Chinese universal order.

The *ch'i-fu* is a schematic diagram of the universe (page 50). The lower border of diagonal bands and rounded billows represents water; at the four axes of the coat, the cardinal points, rise prism-shaped rocks symbolizing the earth mountain. Above is the cloud-filled firmament against which dragons, the symbols of imperial authority, coil and twist. The symbolism is complete only when the coat is worn. The human body becomes the world axis; the neck opening, the gate of heaven or apex of the universe, separates the material world of the coat from the realm of the spiritual represented by the wearer's head.

The *ch'ao-fu* was fully developed by the beginning of the Ch'ing Dynasty, but the fact that the *ch'i-fu* continued to evolve during the first hundred years of Manchu rule suggests that its development took place comparatively late. Before the Manchu conquest the raw materials necessary for its production would have only been provided in the form of presentation silks from the Ming court. It is doubtful whether these were supplied in sufficient quantity before the rise of the Manchu to have permitted experimentation and general acceptance of a new silk form.

Dragon patterns on Ming coats were concentrated into zones to complement the flow of the garment. Dense patterns at the yoke and across the top of the sleeves focused attention on the head, creating a horizontal frame from which the rest of the voluminous coat flowed. The band at the knees emphasized the expanse of the skirt and would have enhanced graceful motion without cutting the sweep of the garment to the floor. The embroidered quatrefoil yoke of an early seventeenth-century yardage of cut and uncut yellow silk velvet illustrates the standard Ming convention of placing a dragon at the centre front and back and looping the bodies over the shoulders (page 41). Billows and prism-shaped mountains define the lower edge of this zone. In the skirt bands, smaller dragons run and twist against clouds with mountain and billow borders below.

In the first stage of Ch'ing evolution the distinctions between zones were discarded and instead the entire coat was treated as a decorative surface. The mountain and billow elements move to the hem of the coat, while the rest of the garment becomes the cloud-filled universe on which dragons are displayed. The only example of this early pattern development in the ROM collections is an archaic survival (page 49). The red colour and wide-sleeved style of this embroidered Chinese bridal coat dating from the late nineteenth century relate it more closely to Ming court attire than to *ch'i-fu*. The ornament preserves an archaic Manchu organization: principal dragons remain coiled over the shoulders, echoing the Ming convention, while smaller dragons, freed from the constriction of narrow bands, are given more prominence at the lower skirts.

In the next stage the position of the elements was modified to focus more attention on the principal ornament. Dragon bodies were uncoiled from the shoulders and extended full-length down the front and back of the *ch'i-fu*. A magnificent early

Unused yardage of cut and uncut yellow velvet with embroidered decoration for an imperial Ming *p'ao* is a unique survival of the prototype from which Manchu dragon-patterned coats evolved. Early seventeenth century.
956.67.2 gift of Mrs. Edgar J. Stone

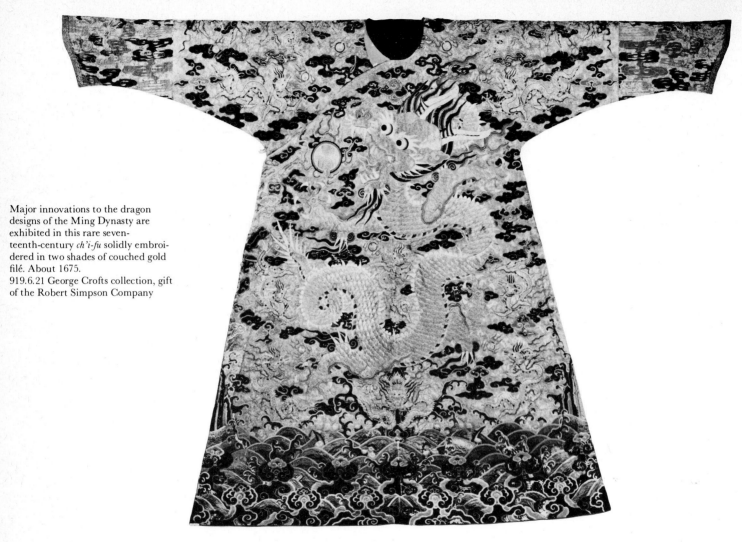

Major innovations to the dragon
designs of the Ming Dynasty are
exhibited in this rare seventeenth-century *ch'i-fu* solidly embroidered in two shades of couched gold
filé. About 1675.
919.6.21 George Crofts collection, gift
of the Robert Simpson Company

example of this type, solidly embroidered in couched gold filé with accents of coloured silk satin stitch, has only two large dragons, shown with semi-profile heads (page 42). They are surrounded by sixteen very small and rather insignificant dragons. The coat has survived without its original cuffs and has withstood at least two alterations. In its present condition the skirts are vented at the sides, and therefore it has been thought to be a consort's coat (Fernald, *Chinese Court Costume*, p. 22). But originally the vents were placed at the front and back in male fashion, making it a coat appropriate for a very exalted Manchu noble, possibly even the K'ang-hsi emperor himself.

Further development is illustrated by a late seventeenth-century tapestry-woven silk and gold filé coat (page 52). Like the previous example it has two principal dragons, facing instead of being shown in profile. A secondary dragon has been added at each shoulder, establishing the Ch'ing convention of four principal dragons radiating from the neck opening. The coat has been recut in Tibetan style, the cuffs have been discarded, and material from the inner flap has been pieced to extend the sleeves and fill in the areas under the arms. The coat may have been sent as yardage to be made up in Tibetan style after relations with the Dalai Lama were established in 1648, or it may have been remodelled from a Manchu coat sent to Tibet during the first quarter of the eighteenth century, after the large-scale dragon patterns had gone out of fashion.

The fact that the *ch'i-fu* was worn tightly belted at the waist, thus cutting the large single dragon designs in half, probably is the reason why dragon patterns were again separated into two zones in the late seventeenth or early eighteenth century. The four larger dragons were confined to the upper part of the coat. Pairs of smaller confronted dragons were placed on the skirts at the front and back, with a fifth placed out of sight on the inner front flap. This symbolic dragon brought the total to nine, a number associated with man in ancient Taoist numerology (Needham, *Science and Civilisation*, p. 271). Changes in scale of the more prominent design element led to changes elsewhere. The lower border of an early eighteenth-century brocaded ivory silk coat takes on added significance as it advances upward to fill the void (page 44). From this point the *li-shui* or standing water, indicated by parallel sets of wavy bands, became a prominent feature of *ch'i-fu* design. Despite these subtle shifts there is little to detract from the major dragon symbol. The decorative emphasis on the circular neck and curved front flap had not yet developed. Visual continuity extends even to the cuffs, which

were made to match the coat.

During the first half of the eighteenth century ever greater refinement was brought to the decoration of the *ch'i-fu*, at the expense of the dragon symbol. The distinction between large and small dragons for the two areas of the coat had largely disappeared by the mid-eighteenth century. Increasing attention was paid to secondary elements. The wave border continued to increase in depth. Cloud forms gradually evolved from larger scattered motifs to the more uniform densities of smaller ribbon-like forms. A plethora of auspicious signs and incidental good-luck symbols also made an appearance.

By mid-century, several changes in construction had also been made. Most early *ch'i-fu* coats whose sleeves have not been altered show no division between upper and lower sleeves, and in fact the cuffs generally continue the same fabric as the body of the garment. In the second quarter of the eighteenth century, two-part sleeves like those of the *ch'ao-fu* were introduced. The dragon design at the shoulder of a mid-eighteenth-century tapestry-woven silk coat has been reduced in length and a ribbed sleeve extension of contrasting fabric has been added (page 53). Cuffs and a band of a second contrasting fabric added to face the neck and top edge of the coat flap emphasize the distinctive construction of the coat at the expense of the decoration.

The imperial edicts promulgated after 1759 at the order of the Ch'ien-lung emperor regulated official dress and accessories for the numerous ranks of an elaborately graded court. The *ch'i-fu* was adopted as the official semi-formal court coat. It was to be worn in public with a short-sleeved, dark-coloured coat on which insignia of rank were displayed. This additional garment probably accounts for the change in *ch'i-fu* sleeve construction. The 1759 edicts were introduced in part to check against increasing Chinese influence, but the adoption of several ancient Chinese style costumes had the effect of de-emphasizing the Manchu nomadic past and relating the Ch'ing Dynasty to native imperial precedents.

The ever more hardened and lifeless forms of nineteenth-century dragon symbols reflected the broader effects of dynastic decay. As the imperial authority waned, so did its ability to control the quality of workmanship, and so did the financial resources necessary to support that work. With the decline of imperial control, minor decorative elements became more and more elaborated at the expense of the symbolic integrity of the dragon (page 45).

Ivory satin *ch'i-fu* brocaded in silks in shades of blue, red, yellow, green, violet, and grey with gold filé and gilt paper strips. The coat is completely machine stitched, suggesting that the piece remained an unused yardage until the twentieth century. About 1725.
956.251 gift of Mrs. Edgar J. Stone

Hardened and lifeless dragon forms on this gold filé embroidered blue silk twill *ch'i-fu* reflect the broader effects of dynastic decline. 1875-1900.
972.358.13 gift of Mrs. Arnold Matthews

46

Evolution of Ch'i-fu

a) Hypothetical reconstruction of skin prototype.

b) Late seventeenth- and early eighteenth-century silk *ch'i-fu* identical in construction to *ch'ang-fu* (ordinary coat) with cuffs of matching material (ROM 965.251, see page 44).

c) A dark surcoat with insignia badges was required wear with the *ch'i-fu* from 1759. Post-1750 *ch'i-fu* with altered sleeve construction. Extensions of dark ribbed fabric, cuffs and facings of contrasting fabric (ROM 911.6.21, see page 53).

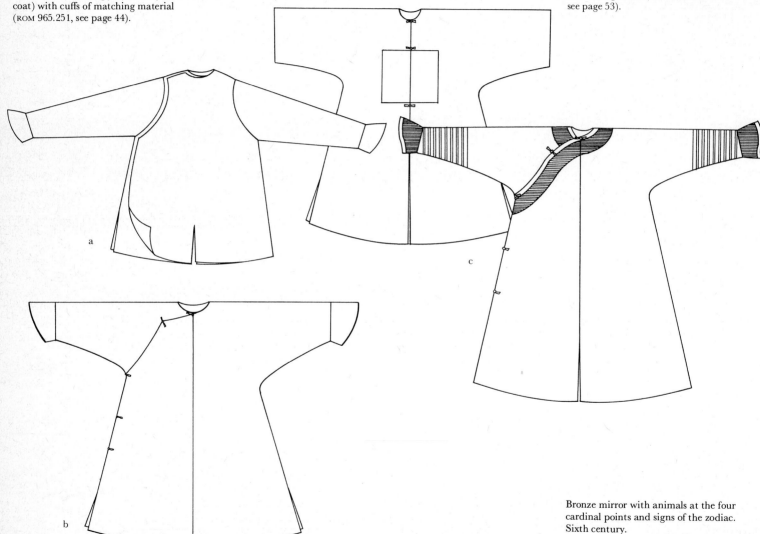

Bronze mirror with animals at the four cardinal points and signs of the zodiac. Sixth century.
Diam. 19.5 cm
928.12.2 Bishop White collection

FIVE COLOURS
OF THE UNIVERSE

48

In ancient Chinese thought, a universal theory based on the five elements (earth, wood, fire, metal, and water) was used to classify and explain natural phenomena. According to this theory, symbolic correlations encompassed every conceivable category of things in the universe. At the centre was earth, its colour yellow; to the east, wood and the colour green (sometimes blue), symbolized by the dragon; to the south was fire, represented by red, symbolized by the phoenix; to the west, metal and the colour white, symbolized by the tiger; and to the north, water and the colour black, symbolized by the tortoise and snake.

Red was associated with family celebrations, particularly weddings and births. Its name, *fu*, is a pun on the word for happiness. Red was also the dynastic colour of the Ming Chinese, and consequently it was largely avoided by the Manchu conquerors. This satin Chinese bridal coat with couched gold filé dragons looping over the shoulder preserves a pre-Manchu construction and style of ornament. About 1875. 919.6.145 George Crofts collection, gift of the Robert Simpson Company

Ch'i-fu decoration is a schematic diagram of the universe. The lower border of diagonal bands and rounded billows represents water; at the four axes of the coat, representing the cardinal points, rise prism-shaped rocks symbolizing the earth mountain. Above is the cloud-filled firmament against which dragons, the symbols of imperial authority, coil and twist. The symbolism is complete only when the coat is worn. The human body becomes the world axis; the neck opening, the gate of heaven or apex of the universe, separates the material world of the coat from the realm of the spiritual, represented by the wearer's head. The greenish-yellow colour of this embroidered satin *ch'i-fu* indicates that it was made for a eunuch serving the imperial household (modern cuff replacements). 1725-1750.
951.142

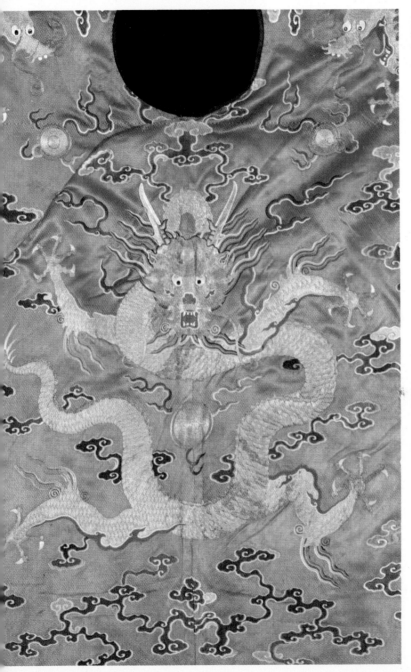

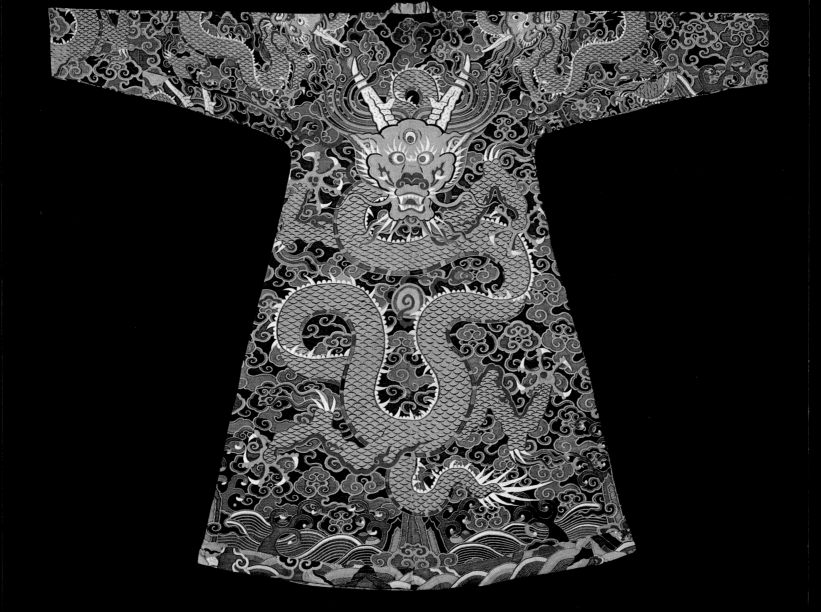

The two shades of metallic gold used for the dragon pattern enhanced the dramatic quality of this coat (left), which was intended to be viewed by artificial light in the early hours before dawn, the time considered most auspicious for court functions. The secondary dragon added at each shoulder established the Ch'ing Dynasty convention of four principal dragons radiating from the neck opening. This early silk and gold filé tapestry-woven *ch'i-fu* survives in a form altered to Tibetan style, with material from the inner flap used to extend the sleeves and fill in the area under the arms. 1675-1700. 974.368

The 1759 edicts governing court costume stipulated that coats for the imperial family should have clouds of five colours as omens of happy augury. Here they are rendered in the more naturalistic pink, pale blue, light green, violet, and dark yellow. This tapestry-woven silk and gold filé *ch'i-fu* exhibits the culmination of eighteenth-century refinement. It shows structural changes to the sleeves and the addition of neck facings. 1750-1775.
919.6.11 George Crofts collection, gift of the Robert Simpson Company

Yellow was the dynastic colour of the Manchu and the clear, bright yellow was reserved for the emperor and his chief consort alone. This emperor's embroidered satin *ch'i-fu* has the twelve ancient symbols of imperial authority which were added to imperial clothing in 1759. Tao-kuang period (1821-1851). 919.6.23 George Crofts collection, gift of the Robert Simpson Company

Square pictorial badges (right), displayed on the back and front of simple three-quarter-length surcoats, distinguished the various ranks of civil and military officials appointed to serve the Dragon Throne. The brilliant colours contrasted sharply with the plain navy blue or black silk coats. Examples from the Krenz collection, gifts of Mrs. Sigmund Samuel.

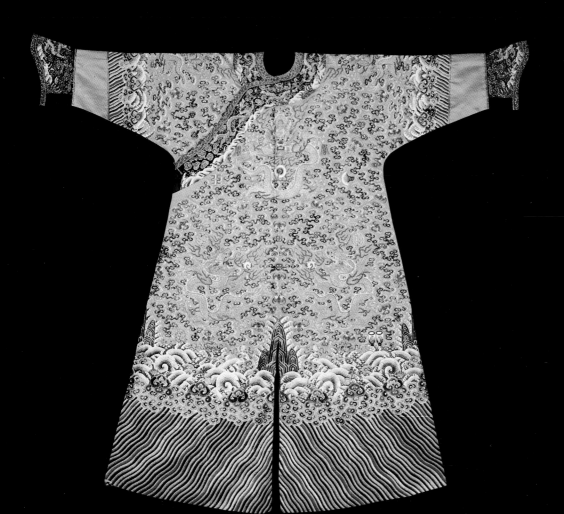

a) Insignia for first-rank civil official (crane). Silk and gold tapestry. About 1700. 950.100.124
b) Insignia for fourth-rank civil official (goose). Tapestry-woven silk. 1750-1775. 950.100.304
c) Insignia for second-rank military official (lion). Tapestry-woven silk. 1750-1800. 950.100.316
d) Insignia for censor (*hsieh-chai:* unicorn). Embroidered silk. 1825-1850. 950.100.47

a

c

b

d

This Manchu woman's embroidered satin coat, reportedly from the wardrobe of the Dowager Empress, Tz'u-hsi, reflects the acceptance of Chinese aesthetic principles. The dark blackish-purple colour, associated with the element water and the direction north, was reserved for winter wear. Here it is matched by delicately coloured narcissus patterns appropriate to the season. 1880-1890.

"The Emperor 'Teou-Kwang' review
his Guards, Palace of Peking"

58

Twelve-Symbol Ch'i-fu

When imperial edict codified Ch'ing court costume in 1759, the emperor's own formal and semi-formal coats were exalted above all others with the addition of the twelve ancient symbols of imperial authority to the basic decorative schema. Following Han Dynasty precedent, this distinction was reserved for the emperor alone. The symbols related to the sacrificial obligations of the emperor and were used on the official clothing of each succeeding dynasty. By taking possession of the ancient symbols of Chinese imperial prerogative, the Ch'ien-lung emperor asserted the mandate of the Manchu imperial clan.

Symbols for the sun and moon at the shoulder and for the constellation and mountain at the chest and back denote the four principal annual sacrifices made by the emperor. The *fu* symbol and axe denote temporal power; the paired dragons and pheasant, dominion over the natural world. The water weed, libation cups, flame, plate of millet, and the mountain at the back symbolize the five elements of nature: water, metal, fire, plant life (by extension, wood), and earth.

Emperor's embroidered yellow silk twill *ch'i-fu*, Ch'ien-lung period (1736-1796), with symbols for the sun (three-legged bird) and the moon (hare).
909.12.2

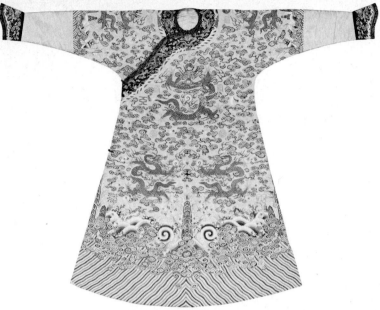

Emperor's yellow silk tapestry-woven
ch'i-fu, Chia-ch'ing period (1796-1821),
with symbols for the earth (mountain)
and the stars (constellation).
971.20.1 gift of Mrs. Edgar J. Stone

Emperor's embroidered yellow satin
ch'i-fu, Tao-kuang period (1821-1851),
with the *fu* character and the axe
symbols.
919.6.23 George Crofts collection, gift
of the Robert Simpson Company

Emperor's blue silk tapestry-woven
ch'i-fu, Hsien-feng period (1851-1862),
with the flowery bird (pheasant) and
the dragon symbols.
919.6.3 George Crofts collection, gift
of the Robert Simpson Company

Emperor's embroidered creamy white satin *ch'i-fu*, Hsien-feng period (1851-1862), with the waterweed and libation cups symbols.
919.6.22 George Crofts collection, gift of the Robert Simpson Company

Child emperor's yellow silk tapestry-woven *ch'i-fu*, early Kuang-hsü period (about 1880), with plate of millet and fire symbols.
910.65.15

After 1759 all courtiers were required
to wear a surcoat over other court
attire; on it were displayed insignia
badges to indicate rank. This posthumous portrait of a seventh-rank civil
official depicts a fur-trimmed hat and
fur-lined *p'u-fu* with mandarin duck
insignia, typical Manchu winter attire.
1875-1900.
115.5 × 63.4 cm
921.1.152

P'u-fu

After 1759 all members of the imperial court from the emperor down to the lowest appointed official were required to wear the *p'u-fu.* This was a plain, dark-coloured, unbelted surcoat designed to be worn over a semi-formal coat. These simple coats were made of two lengths of cloth fashioned with short sleeves, open down the centre front and vented at the sides and back, and were part of the nomadic heritage brought from the north by the Manchu. The coats were worn over other garments but were never finished with the flaring cuffs of the riding coat. For men the coat was invariably three-quarter length, leaving the long cuffed sleeves and decorated hem of the *ch'i-fu* exposed. Women, however, frequently wore full-length surcoats.

Elevation of this particular garment to the rank of court attire achieved several ends. The measure acted as a social leveller, requiring all, regardless of means, to appear at court in similar garb. The very simple construction of the coat made it ideal for displaying the pictorial insignia of rank that had been adopted by the Manchu in 1652. The system of insignia badges followed Chinese precedent, but whereas the Ming had applied the badges to the front and back of their court coats, the short-sleeved nomadic surcoat stressed Manchu national identity. On a less obvious level the garment linked the Manchu to former barbarian dynasties. The Mongol Yuan (1260–1368) wore decorated surcoats as part of their costume; the Jurched Chin, who ruled northern China from 1115 to 1234 and from whom the Manchu claimed descent, also utilized such a surcoat.

Noble ranks were indicated by dragon badges. This embroidered satin emperor's surcoat has four circular insignia. Less exalted ranks were indicated by fewer or square dragon insignia. 1850-1875.
914.7.8

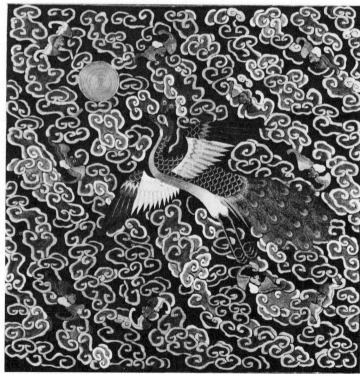

Insignia for civil ranks (all items in
series 950.100 Krenz collection, gift of
Mrs. Sigmund Samuel).

Second rank–golden pheasant, silk
tapestry. 1825-1875.
950.100.247

Third rank–Malay peacock, embroidered. 1875-1900.
950.100.53

Fifth rank–silver pheasant, embroidered. 1875-1900.
950.100.81

Sixth rank–lesser egret, embroidered.
1800-1850.
950.100.208

Seventh rank–mandarin duck, embroidered. 1800-1825.
950.100.178

Eighth rank–quail. The separately
embroidered bird could be changed if
an official advanced in rank. 1900-
1910.
972.163.36 gift of Mrs. William C.
White

Ninth rank–paradise flycatcher,
embroidered. 1850-1875.
950.100.154

Insignia for military ranks.
First rank–*ch'i-lin* (unicorn), embroidered. 1750-1775.
950.100.32

Third rank—leopard, embroidered.
1875-1900.
950.100.12

Fourth rank—tiger, embroidered.
1825-1850.
950.100.184

Fifth rank–bear, brocaded. 1875-1900.
950.100.7

Sixth and seventh ranks–tiger cat
(panther), embroidered. 1875-1900.
950.100.314

Miscellaneous insignia.
Musician–oriole, brocaded. 1750-1800.
950.100.194

Manchu winter court hats were
derived from fur-lined nomadic caps
with upturned brims. The button at
the top indicates rank; the tubular
fitting and peacock feather plume are
a mark of distinction for service to the
throne. 1875-1900.
922.4.26

Court necklaces of 108 beads divided into four sections were based on Buddhist prayer beads. This example features amber and aquamarine with tourmaline, rose quartz, and coral, and was worn with the pendants hanging down the back. 1750-1800. 973.32

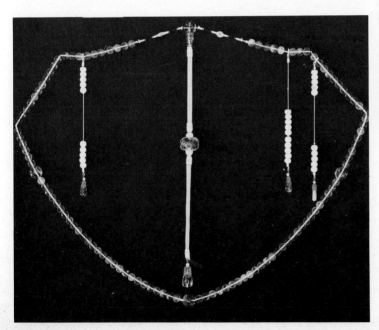

The Manchu summer court hat was based on a conical bamboo sunshade utilized by sedentary peoples of the Chinese plains. 1875-1900. 922.4.29

This embroidered blue satin informal coat is similar in construction to men's coats, but the skirt vents are placed at the sides. This example from the wardrobe of the Dowager Empress, T'zu-hsi, reflects the high standards of workmanship that were maintained for the private court. 1890-1900. 919.6.128 George Crofts collection, gift of the Robert Simpson Company

Ch'ang-fu

Ordinary coats, *ch'ang-fu*, are the same in construction as *ch'i-fu* and probably were the source from which the latter developed. Although these garments were not tied directly to court function, they ranged in style from formal to informal depending upon their use. Male *ch'ang-fu* most closely resembled the riding coat with fitted sleeves and cuffs, vented back and front and worn belted. The long sleeves and cuffs were most often the same colour as the body of the coat. This reinforces the hypothesis that the *ch'ang-fu* was derived from the basic Manchu coat, over which the rest of the festive or ritualistic paraphernalia was worn.

Women's *ch'ang-fu* were slit at the sides and generally worn unbelted. The sleeves were commonly cut wider than men's. Some of the more formal coats had shaped cuffs relating to court styles, but by the late nineteenth century these had become completely debased and were commonly worn turned back. A second sleeve variant, which is frequently seen in collections of Manchu women's wear, has straight wide sleeves faced with contrasting fabric which is turned back to form decorative cuffs.

As auxiliary garments men wore various short and long surcoats. Women had either sleeveless coats in long and short forms or surcoats similar to male costume. Sumptuary laws did not regulate the decoration of these coats. They are among the loveliest of Manchu costume, particularly in the latter part of the Ch'ing Dynasty when much of the formal court attire had lost its vitality. Late Manchu women's informal wear reveals a complete acceptance of Chinese notions of aesthetics which linked colour, fabric, and decoration to seasonal variation.

Blue silk and gold filé tapestry-woven sleeveless coat of the type worn informally by upper-class Manchu women. The angled shoulder seams relate to skin traditions rather than to cloth constructions. 1875-1900.
919.6.84 George Crofts collection, gift of the Robert Simpson Company

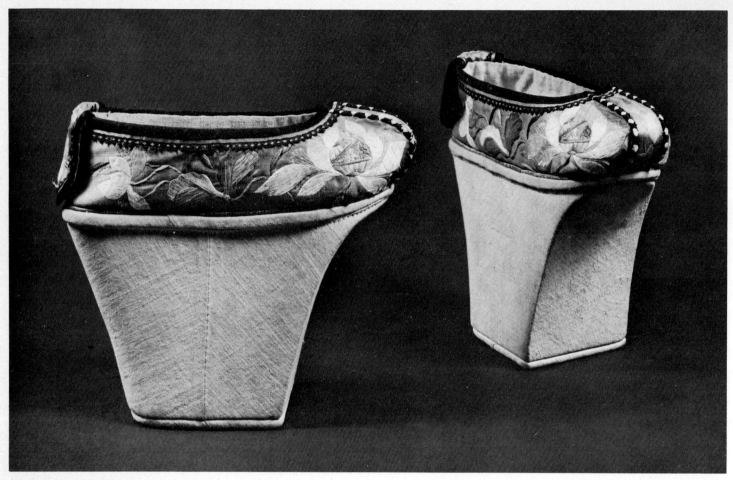

The raised platforms of Manchu women's informal shoes increased stature and gave an impression of smaller feet which were esteemed by the Chinese. Embroidered red satin. 1875-1900.
922.4.72

The black satin constructions of this Manchu woman's headgear represent hair arranged over a frame which supports an ornamental jade bar. Wing-like shapes evoking horns are characteristic of nomadic women's headgear throughout the eastern part of the Eurasian steppe. Both Chinese and Manchu women's hats imitate coiffeurs. Burnham (*Cut My Cote*, p. 29) suggests that elaborate hair dressing was possible because coats were constructed to open down the front, leaving the hair undisturbed. About 1900.
930.9

A Note on Dating

Scholars have isolated the group of twelve-symbol *ch'i-fu* as
having special bearing on the dating of Ch'ing costume, which
is largely undocumented. A system proposed by Alan Priest in
1943, based on careful comparison of the various decorative
elements of these coats, arranged a sequence which was then
assigned to reigns of individual emperors. On the premise that
stylistic changes would emanate from the court and filter
through society, this sequence served as a standard on which to
base stylistic comparisons for other garments. Priest began his
sequence with the reign of the K'ang-hsi emperor, roughly a
century too early, as was pointed out by Helen Fernald in 1946.
Her suggestions for revising the sequence downward, beginning
with the reign of the Ch'ien-lung emperor, were substantiated
and elaborated by Schuyler Cammann in 1952 from his
research on literary evidence. To a large extent the dating
suggested in this catalogue is based on this system. Further
refinement is obviously necessary, particularly for the period
pre-dating the 1759 edict.

THE COLLECTIONS

The collections of Ch'ing period costume are among the more important holdings of the Royal Ontario Museum, paralleling in scope and range some of the other aspects of its important Chinese holdings. The collection of Manchu court costume is among the best public collections anywhere and is particularly distinguished by several unique early Ch'ing coats. Informal attire, although concentrated from the latter part of the dynasty, is comprehensive in range of materials, styles, and techniques, and reflects the broader social strata as well as the rarefied atmosphere of the court.

The first examples of Chinese costume were acquired in 1908–1910 from S.M. Franck, a London dealer. Among them are mid-eighteenth-century pieces associated with the Ch'ien-lung period. These probably came from the summer palaces that were looted during the Boxer Rebellion in 1900.

The core of the collection was acquired between 1919 and 1922. It was purchased on the Peking market by George Crofts, an English fur merchant in Tientsin, who helped the ROM acquire much of its Chinese material. The 1919 shipment of 173 items described by Crofts as "rare to usual" was acquired for the Museum by the Robert Simpson Company. Among them were informal "elaborate Manchu robes of the late Empress Dowager of China and her court ladies", including a very rare early Ch'ing dragon coat and other court attire, and fine silk furnishings. Later Crofts shipments added examples of court and informal accessories, carpets, and embroideries.

From the Museum's founding in 1911, its collections have been built up slowly but continuously, largely through the efforts and generosity of many, many private donors. Missionaries or families of Canadian missionaries, such as Mrs. William C. White, wife of the first Anglican bishop of Honan Province and later first head of the Far Eastern Department of this Museum, contributed material acquired in China which they either wore or were given as presents. This material includes costumes from northern China, particularly Honan, southwestern China, northern Laos, Tibet, and Korea.

Mrs. Davidson Black, wife of the Toronto palaeontologist who discovered Peking Man, being unable to bring money out of China during the Sino-Japanese war, purchased antique clothing and embroideries which made their way to Toronto. Over the years many of "Mrs. Black's coats" have come into the collections after being enjoyed privately.

Other interested individuals, such as Mrs. Edgar J. Stone, have assisted the Museum in acquiring important early and rare examples to increase the scope of the collections, as well as adding outstanding examples of eighteenth-century court garments. In 1950 more than five hundred examples of costume and costume accessories including many court insignia from the Krenz collection were acquired for the Museum by Mrs. Sigmund Samuel, wife of a member of the Museum board whose family has provided long and continuous support for the Museum.

The Museum is also the repository of many church college collections, formed by missionaries and alumni. The Knox College collection acquired in 1915 includes nineteenth-century material from northern China, Korea, and Taiwan. The

Toronto Diocesan Anglican Church Women's collection was transferred in 1971, forming one of the largest single acquisitions in recent years.

The following checklists itemize Ch'ing period costume by types, and give some impression of the range of the ROM's holdings. At least equally important to the study of East Asian costume are collections of related costume from many geographical regions surrounding China. These include: Southeast Asia, the southern Chinese highlands, the Tibetan Plateau, Korea, and the islands extending from Indonesia to the Kuriles. Secondary sources include a large collection of commemorative and posthumous portrait paintings, often referred to as ancestor portraits, and for the earlier periods, sculptural representations of garments on ceramic tomb figures.

I. Manchu court attire

A. *ch'ao-fu* (formal coats):
914.7.7 (female)
949.34.2 (skirt)
950.100.568 (male)
952.106 (male)
966.211.26 (skirt)

B. *ch'i-fu* (semi-formal coats):
1. 17th-century *ch'i-fu*:
919.6.21
974.368

2. 18th-century *ch'i-fu*:
909.12.2 (12 symbol)
919.6.9
919.6.11
919.6.24 (12 sym.)
951.142
953.185
965.251
971.20.1 (12 sym.)

3. 19th-century *ch'i-fu*:
909.12.1
910.65.15 (12 sym.)
910.65.16
914.1.4

914.1.5 (12 sym.)
914.7.2 (12 sym.)
914.7.3 (5 sym.)
914.7.4
918.17.1
919.6.1
919.6.2
919.6.3 (12 sym.)
919.6.4
919.6.10
919.6.12
919.6.13 (5 sym.)
919.6.14
919.6.15
919.6.18
919.6.19
919.6.20
919.6.22 (12 sym.)
919.6.23 (12 sym.)
919.6.38
919.6.46
919.6.52
919.6.56
920.15 (5 sym.)
933.14.9
949.34.1
953.34.1
961.22 (yardage)
962.35 (5 sym., yardage)

963.48.2
970.225
971.192.2
L972.6.8 (12 sym.)
L972.6.9
972.117.33
972.358.13
974.153.1
974.205
974.404.1 (12 sym., yardage)

C. *ch'ang-fu* (informal coats):
919.6.58
919.6.59
919.6.117

D. other dragon coats:
910.65.82
910.65.83
918.17.2 (bridal)
919.6.145 (bridal)
950.100.539 (temple)
950.100.542 (bridal)
952.9 (temple)
969.138.2 (temple)
970.241.3 (temple)

E. *p'u-fu* (surcoats):

1. imperial:
914.7.8
919.6.32
950.100.524 (yardage)
950.100.525 (yardage)
950.100.526
950.100.540 (yardage)
969.258.2
L972.6.7

2. non-imperial:
919.6.29
919.6.40
919.6.148
950.100.527
950.100.535
950.100.545
950.100.547
971.425.1
972.163.4
972.163.8

F. insignia; badges of rank (mandarin squares):
1. noble:
21 examples
2. civil, first rank (crane):
37 examples
3. civil, second rank (golden pheasant):
37 examples
4. civil, third rank (peacock):
27 examples
5. civil, fourth rank (goose):
21 examples
6. civil, fifth rank (silver pheasant):
50 examples
7. civil, sixth rank (egret):
23 examples
8. civil, seventh rank (mandarin duck):
35 examples
9. civil, eighth rank (quail):
11 examples
10. civil, ninth rank (flycatcher):
19 examples

11. military, first rank
(*ch'i-lin*):
19 examples
12. military, second and
third ranks
(lion/leopard):
24 examples
13. military, fourth-sixth
ranks (tiger bear/tiger
cat):
14 examples
14. miscellaneous
insignia:
30 examples

G. *p'i-ling* collars:
954x39
958.5
972.163.27

H. headgear:

1. winter:
914.7.21
922.4.22
922.4.23
922.4.28
939.16.3
948x98
975.110.35

2. summer:
915.3.61
922.4.24
922.4.29
922.4.30
922.4.31
922.4.32
922.4.33
922.4.34
922.4.35
922.4.36
922.4.37
922.4.38

922.4.39
922.4.40
922.20.92
939.16.1
952x103

I. footwear:
915.3.168
918.17.8
919.6.153
922.4.83
922.4.84
922.4.85
946.46.6
975.110.34

II. Manchu unofficial attire

A. women's clothing:
1. coats:
910.65.13
910.65.14
914.7.6
914.7.9
914.7.14
919.6.31
919.6.33
919.6.39
919.6.43
919.6.44
919.6.45
919.6.47
919.6.48
919.6.49
919.6.50
919.6.64
919.6.69
919.6.70
919.6.71
919.6.74
919.6.75
919.6.76
919.6.77
919.6.78
919.6.79

919.6.80
919.6.81
919.6.82
919.6.88
919.6.89
919.6.91
919.6.94
919.6.95
919.6.118
919.6.120
919.6.121
919.6.127
919.6.128
919.6.129
919.6.130
919.6.131
919.6.132
919.6.133
919.6.134
919.6.135
919.6.136
919.6.137
919.6.138
919.6.139
919.6.140
919.6.141
919.6.143
919.6.144
936.12
950.7
950.100.529
952x107
957.153.46
958.107.11
971.115
971.166.69
971.192.5
L972.6.1
L972.6.2

2. long vests:
919.6.28
919.6.84
933.14.11
956.47.1

3. short vests:
910.65.2
910.65.3
910.65.5
910.65.11
919.6.36
919.6.37
919.6.63
919.6.67
919.6.72
919.6.83
919.6.87
919.6.90
919.6.97
919.6.98
919.6.99
919.6.100
919.6.114
950.100.549 (yardage)
958x103
L972.6.6

4. short coats:
910.65.1
910.65.4
910.65.6
910.65.7
910.65.9
914.7.5
914.7.13
919.6.34
919.6.66
919.6.68
919.6.92
919.6.93
919.6.96
919.6.112
919.6.122
919.6.123
919.6.124
919.6.125
919.6.126
930.50.1
950.100.550
952x108

971.166.48
971.166.52
971.166.58
971.166.61
971.166.70
L972.6.5
L972.6.10

5. surcoats:
919.6.119
946.2
967.122.54

6. headgear:
922.4.44
922.4.45
922.4.46
930.9
963.49.1

7. footwear:
912.3
912x28.2
914.7.38
914.7.39
918.17.7
919.6.151
919.6.188
919.6.189
921.2.9
922.4.25
922.4.69
922.4.70
922.4.71
922.4.72
922.4.73
922.4.74
922.4.75
922.4.76
922.4.77
922.4.78
922.4.79
922.4.80

922.4.81
950.234.2
972.163.19

B. men's clothing:
919.6.30
919.6.34
919.6.35
919.6.119
946.2
964.48
967.122.54
970.76.3
972.163.11
975.110.32
975.110.33

III. Chinese unofficial attire

A. women's clothing:

1. coats:
909.12.3
909.12.4
910.65.8
910.65.10
910.65.17
910.65.18
910.65.19
910.65.20
910.65.21
910.65.23
914.1.6
915.6.73
919.6.22
919.6.25
919.6.26
919.6.27
919.6.39
919.6.41
919.6.42
919.6.65
919.6.68
919.6.85
919.6.101

919.6.102
919.6.103
919.6.104
919.6.105
919.6.106
919.6.107
919.6.108
919.6.109
919.6.110
919.6.111
919.6.113
919.6.115
919.6.116
941.11
945.8.2
950.100.541
952x104
956.47.2
957.7.1
964.103
969.237.1
970.76.1
970.76.2
970.92.1
970.345
971.166.51
971.166.67
971.192.2
971.192.4
L972.6.3
L972.6.4
972.163.2
972.163.5
972.163.14
972.163.15
972.210.9
972.210.22
972.324
973.259
975.243.1
975.243.2

2. trousers and leggings:
959.27.3
971.166.52
971.166.61
971.166.66
972.163.16
972.163.17
972.210.18

3. paired aprons:
909.12.5
909.12.6
909.12.7
909.12.34
910.65.24
910.65.25
910.65.26
910.65.27
910.65.28
910.65.29
910.65.30
911.8.77
914.7.15
917.7.3
919.6.146
919.6.147
934.4.267
945.8.3
950.100.530
950.100.531
950.100.532
950.100.533
950.100.534
950.100.557
952x105
956.121.1
959.27.2
960.228
967.122.53
970.181.1
971.166.49
971.166.51
971.166.67
972.117.35
972.163.3

975.110.31
975.382.2
976.134

4. formal vests:
941.10.1
950.100.543
950.100.546
950.100.558
957.153.44

5. headgear:
910.65.80
918.21.380
918.21.381
918.21.382
922.4.41
945.31.1
971.166.46
971.166.71
971.166.72
972.163.6

6. footwear:
911.3.76
914.6.1
915.3.63
915.3.67
915.3.97
921.2.10
946.46.3
946.46.4
946.46.5
946.65
971.166.55
971.166.56
972.413.1
974.138.4

B. men's clothing:
1. coats:
910.65.12
957.153.31
969.166.4
971.166.53
972.163.7
972.163.9
972.163.10

2. headgear:
888.6.58
915.3.92
915.3.93
915.3.145 (hood)
934.2
950.100.548 (hood)
956.33.1
957.153.29
960.62.4
960.193.1 (hood)

3. footwear:
912x28.3
915.3.64
915.3.146
932.9
946.46.2
972.163.1
976.113

C. children's clothing:
898.3.1
910.65.81
914.7.10
914.7.11
914.7.12
914.7.40
915.3.94
915.3.167
915.28.4
919.6.51
919.6.54
919.6.55
919.6.60

919.6.61
919.6.62
931.13.114
946.46.1
946.46.8
948.164.1
960.62.2
960.62.3
970.63.2
970.181.2
971.166.50
971.166.54
971.166.60
971.166.62
971.166.63
971.166.64
971.166.65
972.163.18
972.510.9
972.510.10
972.510.11
972.510.13
972.510.14
974x161.1
975.355.2
975.355.3
975.355.4
975.355.5
975.355.10

D. undergarments:
971.166.57
972.163.12
972.163.13
972.210.1

BIBLIOGRAPHY

Burnham, Dorothy K., *Cut My Cote,* Toronto, Royal Ontario Museum, 1973.

Cammann, Schuyler, "Development of the Mandarin Square", *Harvard Journal of Asian Studies,* vol. 8, 1944, pp. 71-130.

—, *China's Dragon Robes,* New York, Ronald Press, 1952.

Fernald, Helen, *Chinese Court Costumes,* Toronto, Royal Ontario Museum of Archaeology, 1946.

Gervers-Molnar, Veronika, *The Hungarian Szür: An Archaic Mantle of Eurasian Origin,* Toronto, Royal Ontario Museum, 1973.

Hansen, Henny Harald, *Mongol Costume,* Copenhagen, Gyldendalske Boghandel, 1950.

Lattimore, Owen, *Manchuria Cradle of Conflict,* New York, Macmillan, 1932.

—, *Inner Asian Frontiers of China,* New York, American Geographical Society, 1951.

Levin, M.G., and Potopov, L.P., *Historical Ethnographical Atlas of Siberia* (in Russian), USSR Academy of Science, 1961.

Mayers, William Fredrick, *The Chinese Government* (3d ed.), Shanghai, Kelley and Walsh, 1896.

Michael, Franz, *The Origin of Manchu Rule in China,* Baltimore, Johns Hopkins Press, 1942.

Needham, Joseph, *Science and Civilisation in China,* vol. 2, *History and Scientific Thought,* Cambridge, University Press, 1956.

Oxnam, R.B., *Ruling from Horseback,* Chicago, University Press, 1975.

Priest, Alan, *Imperial Robes and Textiles of the Chinese Court,* Minneapolis Institute of Arts, exhibition catalogue, April 13-June 15, 1943.

—, "Prepare for Emperors", *Bulletin of the Metropolitan Museum,* new series, vol. 2, no. 1, 1943, pp. 46-51.

—, *Costumes from the Forbidden City,* New York, Metropolitan Museum of Art, 1945.

Tilke, Max, *Costume Patterns and Design, a Survey of Costume Patterns and Designs of All Periods and Nations from Antiquity to Modern Times,* New York, Praeger, 1957.